Davina Dupree Catches a Crook

Fifth in the Egmont School Series

S K Sheridan

Monday, 1st March

Diary!

Arabella has just told me some REALLY exciting news: we're going to have our first lesson with Dr Adam Aardvark today! #Famous explorer, #can't wait to meet him. Apparently our old geography teacher, Mr Fossil, has gone off to conduct some research on endangered animals for a month, so Mrs Fairchild has drafted Dr Aardvark in as a replacement. BRILLIANT headmistress.com. #I love my school.

Me and Arabella have both got brand new geography folders because it's SUCH a special occasion, (neither of us have met a famous explorer before), mine has black and white zebra stripes all over it and Arabella's is covered in gold and black tiger zig zags, very animal print.com.

I haven't actually *met* Dr Aardvark yet but I already know what he looks like because of all the films and magazines he's been in. He seems *extremely* clever, with big, bushy, white eyebrows and a beard to match, a huge, bald forehead and pale, clever blue eyes. Arabella thinks he looks about sixty years old but I think he might be even older than that, maybe about SEVENTY! To be honest, I'm surprised he's lasted so long and hasn't been eaten by a lion or bitten by a snake or stung by a jellyfish during one of his exotic travels. Dangerous job.com. #Don't think I could do it.

Before he left, Mr Fossil gave us each a book about Dr Aardvark and his travels. My favourite chapter was the one where he talks about living with chimpanzees for a year in the middle of a jungle, learning how to grunt, pick ticks out of a chimpanzee's back and peel a banana with one hand. What a legend! Mega epic.com.

More exciting news is that we've made some new friends, Angel Anderson and Diya Gala, who've moved into the dorm next door to ours. They used to live in the part of Egmont where girls from Rubies House sleep, but that bit of the school is being repainted so they've moved next to us Sapphires girls! TOTALLY groovy.com. They have totally opposite personalities, Angel is very chatty, has short hair and keeps getting told off for calling out in class. Diya is very serious, has long, swishy black hair and is one of the cleverest in our year. I think Arabella might be the *absolute* cleverest but I'm not sure. The one thing Angel and Diya both love is animals – they both want to be vets when they grow up so they can't wait to meet Dr Aardvark and ask him loads of animally questions.

Right, I must go now, Diary, because I haven't had

breakfast yet and I'm absolutely starving – Arabella says Marcel's making cinnamon pancakes today so I'd better run before the other pupils eat them all! Yumsters.com!

Tuesday, 2nd March

Wow, Diary!

Seriously, wow, wow and triple wowzers, that's all I can say.

We had our first lesson with Dr Aardvark this morning, and what a lesson it was! Talk about getting our attention. When we filed into the large geography room, (that has a massive globe hanging from the ceiling which actually LIGHTS UP and SPINS ROUND when the lights are turned off, #SO cool, #wish we had one in our dorm), Dr Aardvark was perched on the teacher's desk with a GIGANTIC snake round his neck, his shock of white hair wobbling wildly above his tanned, leathery face. His sharp, minty-blue eyes bulge out a bit making him look permanently surprised and a bit standoffish. Typically, Cleo and Clarice – the most maddening girls in the school – screamed and ran out when they saw it, #wimps, but the rest of us were FASCINATED.

'Can I touch it, Dr Aardvark?' I said, going closer to him. My cheeks turned really hot, which was a bit embarrassing.

'Yes, yes of course,' Dr Aardvark said in a loud, confident voice. 'Toxic won't bite or even try to strangle you, she's had her rat for the week.' I gingerly put out my hand and stroked the snake's brown and green patterned scales, expecting them to feel slimy. Instead, they were dry and felt like smooth leather.

'Toxic?' Arabella said, coming nearer. 'Is that her name? It sounds a bit scary to me.' Some of the other first years crowded round and put out their hands to touch the snake.

'Nonsense!' Dr Aardvark roared, throwing his head back and dislodging Toxic who hissed with disapproval. 'This old girl's a complete teddy bear, hasn't tried to strangle anyone since 2005. Boa constrictors aren't poisonous, they're only dangerous if they coil round a person and squeeze. Look at the old thing – she's milder than a pussy cat!'

More girls came over to stroke Toxic. Angel yelled loudly when the snake curled round towards her, earning herself a disappointed look from Dr Aardvark. Diya stood back, watching Toxic for a while, before asking our famous explorer all kinds of questions about the snake's natural habitat.

While everyone else was stroking the snake, I had a look at the certificates that had appeared all around the classroom, propped up on bookshelves, cabinets and window sills. "Dr Adam Aardvark, Master of

Animaltology from the University of Cambridge", I read. "Dr Aardvark, Professor of Caring for Rare Species", said another in very swirly writing. "Distinction in Wild Animal Studies from Harvard University", "World Leader in Jungle Experiences", the amazing titles just went on and on. No wonder his bald head is so large, it's tightly packed full with his enormous brain.

'Righty-ho, settle down and all that,' Dr Aardvark chuckled, after everyone who wanted to had stroked Toxic. 'Do sit down now girls, and I'll explain a bit about what we're going to do today.' He put Toxic into a cardboard box and perched back on the desk, looking round at us, his blue eyes mild and friendly.

'Right then,' he said, when we were all quiet. 'As most of you probably know, your headmistress, Mrs Fairchild, made the commendable decision to install me as your new geography teacher when that strange little man, Mr Fossil, fluttered off to write some silly book or other.' Arabella bristled beside me. She's really liked Mr Fossil ever since he took us on an exciting school trip to Ni Island. 'I said yes at once, of course,' Dr Aardvark went on, his rich, fruity tones bouncing off every wall. 'Saying I've taught at Egmont Exclusive Boarding School will no doubt add to my already excellent reputation.' Arabella looked at me and rolled her eyes. I grinned back, hoping she would give him a chance. He probably spends so much time with animals that he's forgotten how to talk properly to humans, poor thing.

'*My* lessons,' Dr Aardvark continued, stroking his beard. 'May be a little *different* to Mr Fossil's. A tad more exciting perhaps and, dare I say it, rather more interesting.' Arabella snorted but I was secretly pleased. I *quite* liked Mr Fossil but he was rather nervous and sometimes I didn't understand what he was saying as he tended to mutter and mumble into his shirt collar. It might be fun to have a more confident teacher.

Cleo and Clarice, I noticed, had sneaked back into the classroom after Toxic had been put in her box and were looking at Dr Aardvark with something close to adoration. Celebrity hunters.com.

'Today,' Dr Aardvark announced. 'You will be learning how to handle grass snakes. Then for homework, I want you to write a one page essay about everything you've learned from me, plus draw a fabulous picture of your snake. I want to see evidence of my *marvellous* teaching.' He beamed, then proceeded to walk round the classroom and hand everyone a wiggly little greeny-brown snake from another, bigger, cardboard box. I was rather pleased to see that mine was much thinner and shorter than Toxic. As soon as Dr Aardvark tried to hand Cleo and Clarice theirs, they screamed and ran out again. #Oh dear, #couldn't help giggling.

Over all it was a really fun lesson, although

Arabella says she prefers Mr Fossil's lessons. I think she'll come round when she's got to know Dr Aardvark a bit better. Angel and Diya are like me, they think he's absolutely amazeballs.

Anyway, must go now, Diary, as it's lunch time and there are delish.com smells coming from the kitchen...

<u>Tuesday Afternoon, 2nd March</u>

Our whole school's gone animal crazy, Diary!

We've just been treated to the most SPECTACULAR animal show EVER! Our resident famous explorer has the most amazing collection of rare and wild animals and birds – and he just showed them to the whole school during assembly!

We were all sitting in the hall in our comfortable armchairs – I don't think I'll EVER get used to how luxurious our school is – when Mrs Fairchild danced out on to the platform at the front. After she'd finished twirling and whirling around, she sang a short song about a buzzy bee, (#SO eccentric, #and I love it!) then introduced Dr Aardvark and his collection of animals.

On came Dr Aardvark, with an eagle perched on his head, a hawk on his shoulder and an eagle on his arm. These are SERIOUSLY big birds, they look like they might be able to pick up someone small, like little Lottie, and fly off with them. Their hooked beaks and sharp eyes gave me the shivers, but I have to say it was most spectacular.com when Dr Aardvark made them all fly around the hall above our heads. A few of the girls were screaming but most of us loved watching the great birds of prey spread their wings and swoop around. When Dr Aardvark gave the signal they all flew back to him and he took them off stage; we all held our breaths wondering what he'd bring on next!

We weren't disappointed – he came back holding

the hand of a chimpanzee, who walked on stage as though he'd been an actor all his life!

'Say hello to Monty,' Dr Aardvark roared, flashing round his best celebrity smile. 'I rescued him from a hunter while living with chimpanzees for a year, no doubt you've all read about it in my book.' Arabella rolled her eyes. I snorted rather loudly.

The show didn't end there; Dr Aardvark brought out Toxic the snake wrapped round his neck, then a baby tiger cub holding a bottle of milk in its paws, then a rare breed of chicken and an enormous furry spider. (Have to admit I didn't really like the last one).

Honestly, what a lot of treats we've already had this term!

Wednesday, 3rd March

Hmm, Diary.

I'm feeling confused.

Yesterday, after school, I took my geography homework to Dr Aardvark's study as I wanted to show him my drawing of a grass snake. Art's my favourite subject and I'd worked on the drawing for AGES, using my new pastels and colouring pencils, getting the scales and colours *just* right. So I was a *little* bit shocked when I knocked on the door and Dr Aardvark said,

'*What*?' In a really snappy way.

'Um,' I said, pushing the door open and going in. Dr Aardvark was leaning back in his gold armchair, sipping a glass of dark red wine. 'I wanted to show you my drawing of a grass snake, Dr Aardark, do you think-'

'Oh for goodness sake! Can't it wait until the lesson?' He growled, his blue eyes looking quite fierce. 'Can't you see I'm very busy? Golly, I hope constant interruptions aren't an aspect of the job. Go away, will you. Show me your little doodle at the end of the next lesson.'

Well! How rude! Can you see why I'm feeling so confused, Diary? How can this brave explorer who was so charming in the lesson suddenly turn so rude? Hmm. Maybe Arabella's right. She says she thinks there's something not quite right about Dr Aardvark but she can't put her finger on exactly what it is.

I'll wait and see what he's like during our next geography lesson before I make up my mind once and for all...

Thursday, 4th March

Worst fears confirmed, Diary.

At first, Dr Aardvark appeared to be back to his usual self at the start of our geography lesson yesterday afternoon. He beamed as we all filed in, Cleo and Clarice making a big deal about strutting across the classroom and swishing their long, blonde hair, pocket mirrors and fold-up hairbrushes clasped tightly in their hands.

The activity Dr Aardvark had planned was quite fun – he'd brought his pet koala bear, Sleepy, with him and we took it in turns to hold her and feed her these green, minty leaves. Sleepy is SO CUTE, but her claws are actually really sharp – I have several scratches down my arm to prove it! After we'd held her we had to research koala bears on our netbooks and write an essay about them on our laptops.

I didn't draw attention to myself throughout the lesson. If I'm honest, I suppose I was still rather offended at Dr Aardvark's outburst the other afternoon. After all, he'd seemed so *friendly* to start with, so heroic – it had been a real shock to be snapped at like that!

Arabella kept nudging me, whispering that I should show Dr Aardvark my drawing and essay about the grass snake. At one point, a group of girls crowded round my folder to look at it and he wandered over to see what all the fuss was about, looking rather annoyed. But his face broke into a big smile when he saw my work. He grabbed my folder and held it up so everyone could see my drawing.

‘Look at this, first years,’ he said, moving the folder around so girls in all parts of the classroom could see it. ‘Young Daphne here came to see me the other night to show me her work, and I’m as impressed with it now as I was then. A shining example of how well I teach, and what great ideas I have. I hope to see work of a similar standard from all of you.’

Most girls grinned at me or gave me the thumbs up sign. Cleo mouthed, “swot” at me and Clarice pulled a mean face, but I wouldn’t expect anything different from them.

But Dr Aardvark’s words had troubled me. “Daphne?”, “ I’m as impressed now as I was then”? The

TRUTH was he couldn't even get my name right and he hadn't been impressed with my work at all the other evening! In fact, been very rude and told me to go away. Could it be that his friendly teacher bit was all an act? I've decided to discuss this with Arabella later. She doesn't like him already because he keeps making unkind remarks about poor Mr Fossil. #Prefer Mr Fossil now, #more real, less fake.

Anyway, Diary, I've got to dash as we're making our own sushi for lunch and Akemi, our tutor, said she'll teach me how to make Unagi Sushi with seaweed and rice! #Yumsters.

Friday, 5th March

Love our new friends, Diary.

Yesterday, me, Arabella, Angel and Diya had a really good chat about Dr Aardvark while we were sprinkling our soy sauce over our sushi.

I told them that unfortunately I now fully agreed with Arabella about Dr Aardvark.

'There's something fishy about him,' I said, munching down on my seaweed roll. 'No pun intended. But I can't explain exactly what.'

'He's a fraud,' Arabella said loudly, licking her fingers, her mass of red hair tumbling about wildly. 'He pretends to be nice then he's rude to people like Davina. And he's so horrible about poor Mr Fossil.'

'Yes,' Diya said, her big, owl eyes looking serious as she picked daintily at her sushi. Everything Diya does is so dainty, I feel like a lumbering elephant just sitting near her. 'But let's not forget about how clever and brave he is, and how he's got so much training from all those universities. I think you were right the other day, Davina, when you said that Dr Aardvark might have spent so much time with animals he's forgotten how to behave politely with humans. I vote we give him another chance.'

'Hmph,' Angel said, stuffing another Kappa Maki into her mouth – Angel seriously loves tuna fish. 'I'm not so sure about him anymore. All he does is tell me off for talking loudly and looks bored if I ask him any questions.

'Well you do have a very loud voice,' Diya said gently.

'Hmph!' Angel said again, consoling herself with another piece of sushi.

I do hope Diya's right about Dr Aardvark and I'm trying to keep an open mind about him, after all, he does bring some really unusual animals to our lessons. But there's something niggling away at the back of my mind...

Anyway, I've got to go to my maths lesson now, Diary, which is NOT good news as we are doing a test.

Saturday, 6th March

Something terrible has happened, Diary!

Mrs Fairchild has been taken very ill!

Basically, Mr Portly, the new deputy head who also teaches us how to use the latest technology, called an emergency assembly this morning. I could tell that something awful had happened because he ran on to the stage on his tiptoes, something he only does if he's VERY stressed. He usually skips if he's happy.

'My dear Egmont girls,' Mr Portly said, looking round at us. 'Something rather, er, perplexing has happened. Your darling headmistress, Mrs Fairchild, was found slumped over her favourite chaise longue early this morning and is now in Little Pineham General Hospital. Her condition is very serious and the doctors are doing all sorts of tests to try and find out the cause.'

Gasps came from all the luxury arm chairs including my own.

'She probably been eating one of her crazy food combinations and got food poisoning,' Clarice whispered loudly, earning herself some very sharp digs in the ribs from surrounding older girls.

I turned to Arabella, feeling a sense of doom and foreboding descend. We both loved Mrs Fairchild very much.

'I was the one to discover Mrs Fairchild,' Mr Portly went on, his high voice rising to a near scream. 'I knocked on her study door to compare notes for this weekend's activities – we were going to offer sky diving and off road biking, both now cancelled until further notice – and found her lying down on the smoky blue chaise longue- at first I thought she was asleep. This seemed strange because as we all know, Mrs Fairchild usually rises with the lark at five each morning. But it soon became clear that she had a raging temperature, I could actually feel heat radiating from her as I went nearer, so I called for an ambulance immediately. She's not usually one for getting illnesses, it really is *very* worrying.'

More intakes of breath as we knew this to be true; Mrs Fairchild was just *always* around, healthy, happy and a bit eccentric. I'd never even known her to have a COLD! Diya and Angel turned and stared at us, their faces as dismayed as I felt.

'But don't worry, dear Egmont girls,' Mr Portly wrung his hands and looked like he was about to burst into tears. 'I'll look after you while poor Mrs Fairchild is in hospital. I'll run the school until she comes back. Oh dear-' he snorted, pulling a blue and white spotted handkerchief out of his pocket and trumpeting into it. 'This really is *too* sad.'

'Poor Mr Portly,' Arabella whispered as we all filed out, most girls looking pale faced. 'He's a kind man but not a natural leader.'

'Let's meet up at lunchtime,' Angel muttered as she passed us. 'We *definitely* need to discuss this!'

Shocking turn of events.com!

Sunday, 7th March

Me, Arabella, Diya and Angel discussed Mrs Fairchild's mysterious illness over our fennel and smoked salmon bagels at lunch yesterday.

'I hate to admit it,' Angel said, chomping away. 'But Clarice could be right. Mrs Fairchild does love to put odd food combinations together – do you remember when she was going round telling everyone that sprout and chocolate sandwiches were just the best thing EVER?'

'Ew yes,' Arabella giggled. 'Davina, do you remember when we knocked on Mrs Fairchild's door to ask for the key to the helicopter warehouse and found her eating tomato, cabbage and sherbet flavoured gravy?'

'Yes,' I smiled, remembering how delighted Mrs Fairchild had looked with this new combination. 'She even offered us some!' We all pulled faces at the thought.

'I wish there was something we could do to help her,' Diya said, picking bits off her bagel and pushing them round her plate. 'Mrs Fairchild is such a sweetie. It's just not the same here without her.'

We had double art in the afternoon – yes! - and Miss Cherry and Miss Wise suggested we all make cards for Mrs Fairchild to cheer her up. I was just in the middle of a really complicated bit, sticking real dried fruit into a flat basket I'd woven out of thin dried straw, getting it ready to stick onto my pink, glittery, FABULOUS 'Get Well Soon' card, when the school microphones were switched on and we could all hear Mr Portly clearing his throat. Each classroom has several pink and white speakers fitted to the ceiling so that if anyone needs to make an announcement we can all hear it at the same time. Quite clever really.com. #amazing what you can do with technology.

'My dear girls,' he began, his voice shaking. 'This is the most effective way I could think of telling you the latest news about our dear Mrs Fairchild. And it's not good I'm afraid.' He paused and we could hear loud sniffing and snorting going on. 'I don't know how to tell you this, so I might as well say it. The doctor's tests have come back and it appears that, I can hardly believe I'm going to say this, Mrs Fairchild has been poisoned.'

I dropped my glue stick. Diya burst into tears and even Miss Wise and Miss Cherry went pale. For once

Clarice and Cleo didn't have any stupid remarks to make, they just stood there with their mouths open.

'I know this must be a shock to all of you,' Mr Portly's voice was getting higher and higher. 'Dear Mrs Pumpernickle has asked me to tell you that if anyone is feeling upset and wants to talk to her about it, her door is always open. I must also warn you, Egmont girls, that there will be a few unfortunate disruptions to our school life over the next few days. Because the doctors haven't yet identified exactly what the poison is or where it came from, the police will soon be arriving here to conduct an investigation into whether or not foul play was involved. Basically this means they want to find out if someone poisoned Mrs Fairchild on purpose. Oh I'm too upset, I can't say anymore...' there was a loud crackling and sniffing then the microphone snapped off.

We stared at each other, mouths open, faces pale. Diya was too shocked to cry any more. Poison Mrs

Fairchild on purpose? But who on EARTH would do a thing like that? She's the sweetest, most lovely lamb in the world.

Miss Wise and Miss Cherry told us to get on with our art if we could, but not to worry if we needed to just sit quietly for a while. I find that doing art makes me feel calmer, so I carried on, not wanting to talk to anybody, Mr Portly's words going round and round in my head. I finished the basket, stuck it on the card and drew lots of extra pictures of flowers and hearts to stick all over it, all the time thinking about Mrs Fairchild. By the time the card was finished, I felt calmer, but I felt ANGRY. If someone thought they could poison Mrs Fairchild and get away with it, they had another think coming. She had always been SO good to me, there was no way I was going to let her down now, when she needed help. I decided right there and then that I was going to do EVERYTHING possible to get to the bottom of this mystery and uncover the truth about the poison, and I was pretty certain Arabella would want to do the same.

Monday, 8th March

Prepare yourself, Diary, there's more shocking news...

Golly, police are literally SWARMING round the school. I found one patrolling the corridor outside our dorm this morning, he gave me such a fright I dropped my silver, sequinned history folder and papers fell out and splatted all over the floor. We've all been interviewed and the police are conducting investigations into what the poison might be and where it came from, not a nice business.com.

Arabella and I had just called an emergency meeting with Diya and Angel in our dorm because we know they love Mrs Fairchild as much as we do and we wanted to know if they wanted to help us do some detective work. They'd just begun to get excited and we were talking about maybe sneaking into Mrs Fairchild's office to look for clues, when there was a THUMP THUMP THUMP on the door. Arabella fell off her bed in shock, although she likes doing that and I think she would have done it anyway, crazy girl.com.

The door opened and a scarred, meaty face appeared.

'Hello girls, I'm Detective Inspector Frank Clifford. I'm looking for Diya Gala and Angel Anderson, we've got reason to believe they might be able to help us with our investigation.'

'I'm Diya and she's Angel,' Diya said pointing at her friend, her big brown eyes trying to read the detective's face. 'I'm not sure how we can help you but we'll certainly try.'

'Come with me please ladies, this is a private matter and Dr Aardvark has kindly said we can use his study to talk things over,' Detective Clifford held the door open wide and beckoned them to come through.

'Listen, what's all this about?' Angel sounded like she was getting stressed so I put my hand on her arm. She has a very fiery temper and I didn't want her to start being rude to a detective, that sort of thing could lead to all SORTS of trouble. 'Can't you talk to us here in front of our friends?'

'Not really,' Detective Clifford scratched his pock marked face. 'You see, we have it on good authority that you two were the last two people to see Mrs Fairchild before she was poisoned. Dr Aardvark has confirmed that he saw both of you entering her study at approximately half past eight the evening before she was taken ill, holding some sort of drink or potion.'

'It wasn't a POTION it was a large mug of hot chocolate,' Angel shouted. I could tell she was scared because her arm was shaking. 'The first years take it in turns to bring Mrs Fairchild her evening drink and we all like doing it because she always gives whoever's done it some yummy biscuits.'

'I can confirm this is all true, Detective,' Diya said, looking more solemn and serious than I've ever seen her look in my life. 'Angel and I made her a double hot chocolate and put squirty cream and marshmallows on the top. Mrs Fairchild was so pleased with it that she gave us three Honeycomb Crunchers each.'

'Ooh, did she really?' Arabella drooled. 'They're SO yummy, the way they're all hard on the outside and gooey inside...' I nudged her hard, this REALLY wasn't the time to be praising biscuits.

'These are all things we need to discuss, girls, so if you would kindly come with me we can all sit down and sort things out,' Detective Clifford sounded kind but very firm. 'You see, as you two were the last people to be seen entering Mrs Fairchild's study with a liquid that we know she drank, I'm afraid to say that at the moment you are our prime suspects.'

'What?' Arabella screeched, as Diya and Angel got up and allowed themselves to be shuffled out of the room looking pale and confused. 'This is RIDICULOUS! Are you seriously suggesting Angel and Diya poisoned Mrs Fairchild?'

'Calm down,' I said to Arabella in a low but very firm voice. 'It won't help them if *we* get in trouble too. We need to help them properly Arabella, so please shut up until Detective Inspector Clifford has gone.'

Tuesday, 9th March

Time for some serious detective work, Diary.

We seem to be facing a crisis at Egmont Exclusive Boarding School for Girls. Yesterday, after Diya and Angel had been taken away for questioning, Arabella and I tried to regroup and assess the situation, which was very difficult because Arabella has a hot temper and kept stomping round the dorm, picking things up and smashing them down again, most distracting.com, #fiery redhead.

'Can you put my new phone down gently please?' I said, feeling rather alarmed when she picked up my amazing new present from my old nanny, Carrie Whepple. It's a phone but has loads of other cool functions, like you can write essays on it and print them off on its mini printer, you can watch television programmes from any country around the world, you can even programme it to smell like a particular place, for example if you press the seaside button wafts of suntan lotion, salty sea, fish and chips and hot sun come out of the phone's speaker. If you press the mountain air button, a crisp, flowery, light scent comes out, it's SO cool.com, # so please don't break my phone Arabella!

'Actually,' I said, thinking fast. 'Can you pass me the phone, no don't chuck it just pass it over, I think Carrie would be gutted if it got broken.'

Arabella sighed and passed it to me, then came and sat down on my enormous bed. I've got my most FAVOURITE duvet cover on at the moment, one with a large photo of me and Arabella on our school trip to Ni Island printed on it. We look really happy but very cold, standing on a desert island in the middle of winter with strange little animals sitting on our feet!

I opened up a new blank typing sheet on my phone. For short bits of writing I like to use my phone but don't worry, dear Diary, it will never replace YOU!

'Right,' I said. 'Let's go through the case so far and I'll write down everything we know. Then it'll become clear what we need to do next to help Mrs Fairchild, Diya and Angel.'

'Good idea,' Arabella grunted, looking slightly

more cheerful. She rolled on to her back. ‘I like having a plan. You’re so good at keeping calm in a crisis, Davina, I don’t know how you do it. So, as far as we all know, this whole thing started on Saturday morning when Mr Portly found Mrs Fairchild. We know that Diya and Angel were probably the last ones to see her and that for some reason Dr Aardvark was very keen for them to be questioned about the poison in his study. To be honest, I wouldn’t be surprised if it was HIM who poisoned poor Mrs Fairchild. Everything was fine until he came to the school and then suddenly our headmistress collapses!’

‘Yes, but Mr Portly’s new too,’ I reminded her, tapping away at the phone’s keypad, recording everything she said. ‘If we are suspecting new people surely we should include him?’

‘Fine, put him on the suspect list,’ Arabella said. ‘But he seems pretty harmless if you ask me.’

I stared at the screen, taking in everything I’d

written. It said: *Suspects so far: Dr Aardvark, Mr Portly, Diya and Angel, (although we don't really think it was them).*

'I reckon we need to do a bit of snooping around in Mrs Fairchild's study,' I said, scratching my head. 'So far we don't have any clues to go on, just a few facts and if we're going to prove Angel and Diya were just in the wrong place at the wrong time and had nothing to do with the poisoning we need hard evidence to back up our claims.'

'Mrs Fairchild's study is being kept locked at the moment and Mr Portly has the key on a big bunch that he attaches to his belt,' Arabella said. 'I saw him locking it up the other day, sniffing and dabbing his eyes. He really is *such* an emotional man.'

'I've just remembered that my old art sketchbook is still in Mrs Fairchild's study,' I said slowly, feeling a plan forming. 'Do you remember Mrs Fairchild borrowing it last week to show to parents who were looking round the school?' Arabella nodded. Mrs Fairchild always asks for a selection of books to show visitors so they can see the kind of work we do here. 'We can go and find Mr Portly and I'll explain that I DESPERATELY need my sketchbook back as there are plans in it that I need to look at for my new art project, which is *kind* of true although I *do* have photocopies, and we can offer to take the key and get the book ourselves as we know how much going back into her study upsets him!'

'I like your thinking, my dear!' Arabella rolled off the bed and stood up. 'Come on then, what are we waiting for? No time like the present, and all that.'

I'll tell you about the unexpected shock we had as a result of all our planning later, Diary – I've got to go now as we've got cooking with Marcel and he's going to show us how to make Ballerina Cakes, yummy.com, then after that we've got Geography with moody Dr Aardvark, boo!

Later that evening, Tuesday 9th March

So anyway Diary,

I'm literally SO FULL right now I can hardly move! The Ballerina Cakes were SO amazing. They went up in layers like wedding cakes, but each layer was part of the ballerina's skirt made from floaty pink and white sugar paper. We made the body and head out of different coloured marzipan and icing, then Marcel showed us how to put it all together. Mine was a bit wonky but she still looked impressive and she smelled all sweet and almondy. I took some photos on my flash new phone to show Carrie, then Marcel said we could eat some of our cakes before Geography. #Ate too much, #will never have to eat again, #can't move or walk properly now.

But anyway, back to detective business. So yesterday afternoon, Arabella and I went off to find Mr Portly, who was changing some fairy-light bulbs in the dining room, (Mr Portly LOVES lights, bless him, he's always adding to the atmosphere of Egmont by installing newer and more glittery ones in every room possible). We told him about my sketchbook and at first he looked horrified when he thought we wanted him to go back into Mrs Fairchild's study.

'Oh I can't girls, I'm terribly sorry,' he held his hand against his heart and went pale. 'That room holds *such* bad memories for me, *poor* Mrs Fairchild was lying there on the chaise longue so quietly, so still. Oh dear me-' He took out a giant handkerchief and blew his nose into it.

'Don't worry Mr Portly,' Arabella said cheerfully. 'Davina and I don't mind going to get the sketchbook, no need for you to go back into that study at all.'

'Oh you *dear* girls,' Mr Portly regained some colour

in his cheeks and fumbled around on the giant key ring around his waist. 'You brave soldiers. Here's the key, give it a jolly good twist, the lock can be quite stiff sometimes.'

So soon, Arabella and I were safely inside Mrs Fairchild's study, ALONE!

'Come on,' I said, immediately spotting my sketchbook on a bookshelf and putting it next to the door so I didn't forget it. 'Let's have a look round for anything unusual, anything that looks out of place or like it doesn't belong here. I reckon we've been in Mrs Fairchild's study enough times to recognize where everything should be, don't you?'

Arabella nodded and we set to work, examining the desk, shelves, cabinets, cupboards and especially the chaise longue. Mrs Fairchild does keep some odd things around but then we've always known that, so we didn't pay much attention to the pair of bongo drums, the book about cheerleading or the row of fancy dress outfits.

'Hang on, what's this?' Arabella turned round from the drinks cabinet next to the chaise longue, holding a beautiful, small pink bottle with a label hanging from its neck. 'I don't remember this being here before, do you?'

'No, I would have remembered it because it's so pretty. Is there anything written on the label?' I said, going over.

'"To Dearest Mrs Fairchild"', Arabella read. '"A small gift from a grateful new employee. I'm so excited to be working at Egmont now and hope to serve you and the girls well as your new deputy head. I shall always cherish the day your letter arrived telling me I'd got my dream job. With best wishes and much admiration, your faithful servant Clarence Portly". It's from Mr Portly and look, it's only half full!'

'Mrs Fairchild must have drunk half already,' I took

the bottle and turned it round in my hands, reading the ingredients. 'It says it's dessert wine.' I took the stopper out and smelled it. 'Ew, very sweet. But Mr Portly's such a sensitive soul, you don't really think-'

At that moment the study door crashed open and Detective Inspector Clifford strode in. He was NOT looking amused.

'Girls! What on earth are you doing in here?' He barked. 'I thought I heard chatting. This room is strictly off limits to pupils, it's the crime scene for goodness sake.' He arrived next to me and yanked the pink bottle out of my hands, very rudely I thought.

'What have we here?' He growled, reading the dangling label. 'Hmm, very interesting. Very interesting indeed. Why didn't my men find this when they did their search?'

Arabella and I shook our heads and looked confused. How on earth were we supposed to know the answer to that!

'I'll bag this and take it down to the police station for testing,' Detective Clifford said, glaring at us. 'And I have a feeling your deputy head will be accompanying me to help us with our enquiries. And from now on, you two meddling kids stay AWAY from the crime scene. Do you understand?'

Arabella looked sulky, like she was about to say something rude, so I quickly said,

'Yes Detective, we just came in to get my sketchbook and noticed the bottle because we thought it looked pretty. Never mind, no harm done, we'll be off now.' Arabella growled under her breath as I dragged her out of the study. No point in annoying Detective Clifford or he might get in the way and stop our secret detective work.

So there we are. We now have more questions than answers and will be having a meeting with Diya and

Angel this evening to see how they are, discuss our findings, and try and work out our next course of action!

Wednesday, 10th March

Some good and bad news, Diary...

The good news is that we've heard Mrs Fairchild's condition has improved and it looks like she'll make a full recovery, although she'll have to rest in hospital for a few more days. Mrs Pumpernickle, our housemistress, bustled around at breakfast time giving everyone the good news. The bad news is that Detective Clifford has arrested poor Mr Portly for not telling him about the wine he gave Mrs Fairchild and is keeping him down at the police station for questioning (although the good bit of this is that Diya and Angel are now no longer the prime suspects), so now Mrs Pumpernickle is acting headmistress, which is making her very cross and flustered.

We had Geography again today and I have to say that Dr Aardvark is looking more tired than usual. Maybe his animals are keeping him up at night or something? He wasn't even that rude when we were asking him questions about his collection of stag beetles, which was a nice surprise.

Cleo and Clarice watched out of the window during Geography when Mr Portly was being led away in hysterics. I couldn't help overhearing the rather mean things they were saying about him.

'I *knew* it was him all the time,' Cleo whispered loudly. 'I *knew* he poisoned Mrs Fairchild right from day one. He's got a long nose and you can't trust people with long noses, Mummy always says.'

'Your nose is *extremely* long, Cleo,' Arabella said loudly. 'Does that mean we can't trust you?'

'It is NOT!' Cleo screamed, turning round. 'My nose is NOT long, is it Clarice?'

'No, it's a very pretty nose, much nicer than old stubby, freckly nose over *there*,' Clarice glared at Arabella. She snapped open her faithful pocket mirror and she and Cleo spent a happy five minutes studying their noses and complimenting each other's. Dr Aardvark didn't even notice!

Diya, Angel, Arabella and I held an emergency meeting last night and decided we needed to snoop round the school to look for more clues when the police wouldn't be hanging around and getting in our way. None of us believe Mr Portly is the poisoner, he's too much of a softie. He likes soft lighting and even keeps a teddy bear on his bed for goodness sake, Arabella and I saw it once when we had to knock on his bedroom door when one of the girls wasn't feeling well in the night. So we've decided that tonight is snooping, detecting night, Diary. The police always clock off at six each evening and don't return until nine the following morning carrying their sausage and egg muffins, so we should be safe. I'll report back tomorrow Diary, #bit nervous, #hope we don't get caught...

Thursday, 11th March

Gob-smackingly unbelievable nightly antics, Diary!

Listen, you are SO never going to believe this...Last night, as planned, me, Arabella, Angel and Diya all set our alarms for midnight. This was a good plan as it meant we got a few hours sleep before our adventure. Arabella and I had dressed in black before going to bed, as planned, so that it would be easier to blend into shadowy areas of the school if we heard anyone coming. We then knocked for Diya and Angel, who were also wearing black and rubbing their eyes, then set off down the softly lit, squishily carpeted corridors towards the main part of the school. We didn't know exactly what we were looking for, we just knew we had to find SOMETHING that pointed to who REALLY poisoned Mrs

Fairchild.

As we rounded the corner into the main entrance hall, where two spiral staircases cascade down either side of an ornate indoor balcony, I put my finger to my lips.

'Shh,' I said. 'Listen. What's that noise?'

We all stood still, holding our breath.

'Cluck cluck CLUUCKK!' Came the noise again.

'A chicken?' Arabella turned to me, eyes the size of golf balls. 'Did you hear that too or am I going mad?'

'We all heard it,' Diya whispered, frowning. 'There's something strange going on here. Let's investigate.' So we tiptoed forwards, not sure what to expect.

'Well I can't *see* a chick-' Arabella stopped as an unusual looking chicken launched itself at her feet from behind a pillar, settling down on her furry slipper with a few contented ‘clucks’.

‘That chicken looks familiar,’ Angel said quite loudly. She finds it difficult to whisper. ‘I know! It’s the one Dr Aardvark brought out on stage the other day, when he was doing his animal show. Do you remember?’

‘Yes!’ I whispered back. ‘You’re right. What did he say her name was?’

‘Mrs Peck,’ Diya said, and Mrs Peck clucked contentedly at the mention of her name.

‘But the question is,’ Arabella said, bending down to stroke Mrs Peck’s feathers. ‘Why on earth is she roaming round the school in the middle of the night? Mrs Pumpernickle said that Mrs Fairchild gave Dr Aardvark and his animals a suite of specially equipped rooms to live in next to his study, surely she should be there?’

‘Maybe she escaped,’ I said. ‘Hang on, if she got out, does that mean some of Dr Aardvark’s other, slightly more...er...scary animals might have escaped too?’

CRASH!

‘AGGHHH!’ Angel screamed. ‘What on EARTH was that?’

‘Huuu! Aaaa!’ Someone said in my ear, then hairy arms wrapped themselves tightly round my neck.

‘Help!’ I shrieked, wondering why no one else was looking alarmed. ‘I’m being attacked.’

‘Don’t worry,’ Arabella grinned. ‘It’s only Monty, Dr Aardvark’s chimpanzee. He just jumped off the balcony and landed behind you. I think he likes you, Davina.’

‘Hello Monty,’ Diya said, coming over, her eyes full of curiosity. ‘Gosh, isn’t he lovely? I think he’s quite young. Look, he’s trying to groom Davina’s hair.’

‘Um,’ I said, trying to act as though I’d always wanted a chimpanzee to groom my hair even though it was starting to hurt. ‘Maybe we could move on now?’

So we did. Monty really seemed to have taken a shine to me for some reason and insisted on walking on all fours right next to me. Mrs Peck seemed rather attached to Arabella as she refused to get off her slipper, so Arabella decided the best thing to do was to walk very slowly, with Mrs Peck happily clucking away.

At one point, after we’d walked right through the entrance hall and were heading down a corridor towards the classrooms, several large, exotic looking spiders zoomed past us, which made me jump but Angel hung back to study them.

‘What’s that?’ Diya said, pointing to a mound of fur on a nearby bookshelf. By the light of the flickering wall lantern I could see that the fur was a soft, grey colour. Suddenly, it snored.

'I think its Sleepy the Koala Bear,' I said, going over to stroke her fur. 'She's *such* a sweetie.'

'Wrraa!' Monty said, looking seriously annoyed.

Sorry Monty,' I turned and stroked his arm. 'Obviously not as sweet as *you*.'

BANG!

'What was that noise?' Angel whispered really loudly, catching up with us, a giant, scary looking spider on the back of her hand.

'I think it was a door closing,' Diya whispered. 'I can hear someone coming. Quick, let's hide.'

So like true detectives we melted away into the dark shadows of the corridor, me and Monty ended up behind a large stone pillar. I held his hand, hoping he wouldn't make a sound.

I stopped being able to breathe as footsteps approached, then stared in amazement as Dr Aardvark, wearing striped pyjamas and looking VERY stressed, came into view. He had a whistle on a piece of string round his neck, which he proceeded to blow softly.

'Dratted animals,' he said, letting go of the whistle and tearing at his hair. 'Where can they have got to *this* time? Monty! Sleepy! Mrs Peck! Come out this instant.' I stared at Monty in alarm in case he was about to blow our cover, but he happily ignored his owner, content to groom my now even more tangled hair. 'I know you must be somewhere...' Dr Aardvark continued, then off he went down the corridor, looking from left to right, blowing his whistle softly, tearing at his hair with his free hand.

Everything was quiet for a few more minutes. No one wanted to move, just in case he came back.

'Ouch,' Angel said loudly. 'I'm sorry but I can't stay squashed up like this any longer, my knees are killing me.' Monty and I came out from behind our pillar in time to see her crawl out of a low cupboard. Everyone else gradually reappeared.

'Well one thing's for sure,' Arabella said, dryly. 'The great adventurer, Dr Aardvark, certainly doesn't seem to have much control over his flock of animals, which seems somewhat strange, don't you think? I would have thought someone who'd lived with chimpanzees for a year would be experienced enough to stop them escaping in the night, but did you hear he said, "where can they have got to THIS time", as though they'd all escaped before.'

'Yes,' I said, holding Monty's hand. 'He did seem rather stressed and out of sorts.'

'Listen,' Diya held her finger up to her lips. We listened and heard a shaking sound accompanied by returning footsteps.

'Food time,' Dr Aardvark's voice came echoing down the corridor. 'Come on out, you dratted animals and have some FOOD!'

Me, Arabella, Diya and Angel quickly sank back into our hiding places, but at the mention of food the animals were off. Even Sleepy sat up and slid off the bookshelf, making her way slowly towards the shaking sound. Within seconds Dr Aardvark was marching back past, and I risked a quick look from behind the pillar and was SHOCKED to see that he wasn't shaking animal feed, he was shaking a box of Choc Pops, CHOCOLATE CEREAL FOR CHILDREN! Surely he didn't feed his collection of wild animals chocolate cereal? But Monty, Sleepy, Mrs Peck, a small tiger cub who thankfully must have been hiding somewhere else, several snakes and a few spiders were padding and slithering behind the now triumphant looking Dr Aardvark, looking very excited about the Choc Pops.

Anyway, Diary, to cut a long story short we all decided to head straight back to our dorms once the tribe of animals was safely out of sight, feeling we'd had more than enough adventures for one night.

I have to go now, Diary, as I'm still rather tired.com after yesterday, in fact I can't keep my eyes open any longer....Zzzzzzz..............

Friday, 12th March

A disappearance, Diary!

You'll never guess what's happened this morning. Arabella, Diya, Angel and I arrived a bit late for our geography lesson as Angel had lost her geography folder and we searched high and low for it before Diya found it stuffed behind a chest of drawers. We were expecting some sharp words from Dr Aardvark for being late but we were surprised to see that he wasn't there. All the other first years were lounging around on desks, chatting to each other - typically Cleo and Clarice were in the centre of the classroom reapplying their make-up, talking loudly.

‘Where’s Dr Aardvark?’ I asked Melody, settling myself down next to her on the edge of her desk. ‘Has he gone out to get some weird and wonderful animal to show us?’

‘He hasn’t turned up yet,’ Melody said, swinging her long legs. ‘We thought he might be ill or something, but no other teacher’s arrived to cover the class yet.’

‘Hmm,’ Arabella said, scratching her nose. ‘I suppose he *has* been looking rather tired all week. Oh I wish Mr Fossil would come back.’

‘Why do you want THAT rat-faced little pip-squeak to come back?’ Clarice yelled from behind her mirror. ‘Dr Aardvark’s *much* more glamorous and he’s *so* well travelled. But then you and Davina wouldn’t know what glamour was even if it hit you in the face, would you Freckles?’

'Why you horrible little-' Arabella began, rising to the bait as usual, getting up to go over to the swishy haired pair, no doubt to give them a piece of her mind.

'Don't rise to their rudeness,' I whispered, dragging her back. 'They're a pair of idiots. Don't give them the satisfaction of seeing that they've upset you.'

The twins, Moira and Lynne, stood up.

'We're going to find Mrs Pumpernickle and tell her Dr Aardvark's not here yet,' Moira said, heading for the door. 'He's obviously not coming and we don't feel like sitting here for an hour listening to Cleo and Clarice be rude to people.'

'SWOTS!' Clarice yelled to their disappearing backs.

Within minutes the twins were back, followed by a *very* flustered looking Mrs Pumpernickle.

'Honestly,' she clucked as she bustled in, her hair coming out of its bun in wisps. 'I don't know what's happened to this school lately, every day something seems to go wrong. Right, where's Dr Aardvark?'

'He hasn't turned up yet,' I explained. 'Is he ill?'

'Goodness I hope not,'Mrs Pumpernickle fussed round the classroom, straightening chairs and indicating to everyone to sit down and face the front. 'He certainly hasn't told me if he is, which is a bit naughty, as every teacher knows they need to tell me as soon as possible if they can't teach a class, so I can find a cover teacher in time.'

Arabella leaned towards me. 'Do you think we should tell her about DR Aardvark and his animals running round the school the other night?' She whispered in my ear. I thought, then nodded. If there was something not right about Dr Aardvark then it was our duty to tell Mrs Pumpernickle everything we knew. I put my hand up.

'What is it, Davina?' Mrs Pumpernickle looked at

me with glazed eyes as she hurried back towards the door. 'Need to go and get another teacher,' she muttered under her breath. 'Is that what you do in these situations? How on earth would I know, I'm not a trained teacher for goodness sake, I'm a house mistress. Why am I acting deputy head? The whole school's gone barking mad...'

'Mrs Pumpernickle!' I said in a louder voice. 'I need to tell you something.'

'Can't it wait?' She got to the door and bustled out of it. 'You can see I'm rather busy at the moment, Davina dear. So much responsibility, a whole school to run and what with teachers disappearing by the minute... Oh dear oh dear, whatever am I to do?' And with that she'd gone, bustling off down the corridor, shaking her head and tutting.

'Right, that's it.' Arabella turned to me, her eyes gleaming. 'I can't help thinking that Dr Aardvark's disappearance and the poisoning of Mrs Fairchild are somehow linked. It's time to take matters in to our own hands.'

Right, I've got to go now Diary, as we are about to put Arabella's rather scary.com plan into action...

Later that evening, Friday, 12th March

A result, Diary!!

Basically, Arabella and I decided we should put her plan into action during break time yesterday afternoon. Unfortunately Diya and Angel had been taken off for more questioning by Detective Clifford, after some tests came back revealing that the milk in the hot chocolate they'd given Mrs Fairchild the night before she was taken ill was ever so slightly off, so they couldn't come with us. Arabella said she'd already noticed some fresh animally signs around the school, like a pile of feathers and an egg behind a staircase and some grey fur caught on the edge of a shelf, and she dragged me round to show me the evidence. I picked up the egg and noticed there was another not far off so went and picked that one up too.

'This one's still warm,' I said, handing it to Arabella. 'Mrs Peck must be quite near. I think you're right, Arabella, Dr Aardvark must still be in the building somewhere if his animals are around, I don't think even he would abandon them.'

Arabella nodded.

'Look,' she said, pointing. 'Is that another egg half way up the staircase? It is! Ew, it's a bit cracked and it's leaking on to the step. Ooh, I wonder if Mrs Peck left a trail of eggs when she was returning to wherever Dr Aardvark is? Come on, let's follow them and see.'

So we did. Mrs Peck had been hugely helpful and laid eggs at regular intervals down several corridors and up two more flights of stairs.

'Blimey,' Arabella smiled, picking up the ninth we'd found. 'We should give these to Marcel and he can make us all omelettes for dinner.'

As we reached the top floor of the school, feeling a bit puffed out, I was worried the trail had gone cold.

'I can't see any more eggs,' I said peering at the floor. The edges of the corridors were rather dusty and cobwebby. Arabella strode over and tried to open the door to the south turret.

'Locked,' she said, rattling it hard. 'And there's dust all around the key hole. It doesn't look like anyone's opened that door for years.'

'Hang on, is that another door a bit further down there?' I said, walking the opposite way down the corridor. 'Yes it is, and the keyhole isn't rusty at all.'

'Try the handle,' Arabella said, bending down to

place her armful of eggs carefully next to the turret door before jogging over. I seized the handle and was just about to yank it down when a voice came from inside.

'Help me, someone!'

'Is that Dr Aardvark?' I said loudly, pushing the handle down quickly. It was a bit stiff but I managed it eventually. The door turned out not to be locked and swung open easily.

'What in the-' Arabella began, then stopped, too shocked to speak.

A scene of utter mess greeted us. A very different looking Dr Aardvark was lying on an old mattress in the middle of a grey, dusty attic. His hair was now greasy and plastered down the sides of his face, which had gone pale and thin. His crazy collection of animals lay and sat around him looking very depressed. Monty the chimpanzee got to his feet and wandered over to us slowly, making sad "oo" noises. The old attic floorboards were strewn with animal poo, feathers and fur, which Monty was now walking through. The smell was TOO HORRIBLE for words and I pinched my nose to block out the worst of it.

'Dr Aardvark!' Arabella said. 'What on earth are you all doing up here? I thought Mrs Fairchild had provided a specially equipped suite of rooms for you and your animals? Why aren't you all there?'

'It's all gone horribly wrong,' Dr Aardvark snivelled, clutching at his arm. He didn't look like an adventurous hero now, more like a whiny school boy. 'I don't like these animals anymore, I want someone to come and take them all away. We all came to hide up here after I realized it was my Brazilian Wandering Spider, Lethal, who'd poisoned Mrs Fairchild by biting her.' Arabella and I gasped. 'She escaped one night after Monty opened the door when I was asleep - he's such a stupid animal, he even does that up here in the attic. I didn't realize she was missing straight away, as I don't really like spiders so I try not to check my spider collection regularly. But when I realized she'd gone – and I'm guessing that oaf Monty let her out when I wasn't looking – I went hunting round the school and found her crawling out from underneath Mrs Fairchild's study door. It doesn't take a genius to work out what happened, does it?'

'But why did you come and hide up here, Dr Aardvark?' I asked, feeling confused. 'Why didn't you do the right thing and own up to what had happened?'

'Because, you stupid child, I'm not the REAL Dr Aardvark, am I? I'm just someone who looks a bit like him - Eddie Barrow's my real name. I didn't want the police to start sniffing about, asking me awkward questions, because I thought they might realize I don't have the right licenses, qualifications or training to be looking after any of these blasted animals. The *real* Dr

Aardvark lives in South America, which you bunch of idiots would have realized if you'd done your research properly.'

'What?' Arabella shrieked, stepping forwards. 'You mean you're a fraud? And all this time you've had the cheek to accuse poor Mr Fossil of being a rubbish teacher! At least he's a REAL teacher with REAL qualifications.'

'Whatever,' Eddie Barrow spat, clutching his arm tighter. 'When I saw the advert in the paper for a geography teacher at posh old Egmont Exclusive Boarding School for Girls, I knew it would pay better money than gutting fish, which is what I used to do before. Everyone always said I looked like the famous explorer, Dr Aardvark, so I thought – why not give it a go? Why not pretend to be him and see if I can't get myself a well-paid job? So I got in touch with friend of mine who's a bit of a dodgy fellow and can get anything anyone wants at the right price, if you know what I mean, and he somehow got hold of this collection of animals for me. And you're all so stupid you fell for it!'

'You rotten crook!' I said, wishing a policeman was here listening to Eddie Barrow's appalling confession. 'So why are you just lying around, clutching your arm, telling us all this? Surely you've just blown your cover?'

'I'm telling you all this,' Eddie said. 'Because my stupid Brazilian Wandering Spider, Lethal, went and bit ME two days ago and now I feel so ill I can't get up.'

'Serves you right,' Arabella said, her face as hard as stone.

'Look, just go and get help, will you? I haven't had a drink for twenty four hours now and I'm parched,' Eddie wheedled.

'So haven't the animals had a drink for that long either?' I asked, eying the empty chocolate cereal packets lying around the room.

'No and they've finished all the cereal too. I love Choc Pops and they're so greedy they eat more than their fair share. But who cares about them? *I'm* the important one here, *I'm* the one that needs saving,' Eddie Barrow said, sounding mega pathetic. 'I don't even *like* animals. When I get out of here I don't ever want to see another one again.'

'You are the most rotten, awful, pathetic, horrible person I've ever met,' Arabella said, her red curls boinging around with fury. 'We ARE going to get help, not for you but for these poor animals who've obviously been neglected and badly treated. You don't feed wild animals and birds chocolate cereal for goodness sake! It could make them really ill. It could –'

'What's going on here then?' Detective Clifford's voice roared through the attic as he came striding in, his face as angry as a thunder cloud.

He stopped and stared, taking in the unlikely scene in front of him.

'Girls, you have three minutes to explain to me EXACTLY what is going on here,' he said, turning to face us.

So we did, not leaving out ANYTHING, and when we'd finished Detective Clifford took out his handcuffs and strode towards Eddie Barrow.

'Get up,' he commanded. 'You're coming with me, you snivelling idiot. If you're lucky I might swing past the hospital to get that spider bite looked at, not that you deserve such treatment. You're a fraudster and a cheat, sir!'

"Cluck!' Mrs Peck said, sitting on Arabella's foot.

Saturday, 13th March

Unexpected ending, Diary!

We just had the most SURPRISING and AMAZING geography lesson in the whole world, Diary. Not only because it was on a Saturday and we don't usually have normal lessons on a Saturday!

Basically, Mrs Pumpernickle bustled over to all the first year tables at breakfast and told us to go straight to the geography room at nine o'clock sharp, no latecomers please. Arabella was a bit worried in case they'd hired an even worse teacher than Eddie Barrows but we had a nice surprise when we entered the room. Dear old twitchy, funny Mr Fossil was sitting there on the edge of his desk, smiling shyly. A roar of appreciation went up as soon as we saw him, (led by Arabella of course, she shouted really loudly in my ear). He blushed and fidgeted even more, but looked really pleased to have such a greeting.

'Hello First Years,' he said, his nose twitching like a rabbit's. 'I had a call from a rather important lady last night, beseeching me to come back from Ni Island earlier than planned. She explained everything about Dr Aardvark, or should I say, Eddie Barrows.'

'What important lady?' Clarice shouted. 'Mrs Pumpernickle's not that important.'

'Oh thanks very much,' Mrs Pumpernickle huffed, who was standing at the back of the classroom wearing her frilly apron, arms folded. 'Now I know who NOT to give seconds to at dinner time, Clarice.'

'I wasn't referring to our much valued and incredibly *important* Mrs Pumpernickle, who I hear has been doing a marvellous job running the school since both the head and deputy were deemed out of action,' Mr Fossil smiled kindly at Mrs Pumpernickle, who stopped tutting under her breath and grinned instead. 'I was referring to the lady we are more accustomed to see running the school.'

'But Mrs Fairchild's in hospital,' Cleo said loudly.

'Everyone knows that.'

'Oh am I?' Said a familiar, light voice that had a touch of cheekiness about it. 'Perhaps "everyone" doesn't know as much as they think, Cleo.'

To our UTTER ASTONISHMENT.COM Mrs Fairchild appeared from round the corner of the big cupboard that houses geography maps, books and supplies. She was sitting very elegantly in a beautiful pale pink wheelchair, a light purple, cashmere blanket covering her knees. Even more surprisingly, the wheelchair was being pushed by Mr Portly.

'Hello dear First Years,' she said, smiling her twinkly smile, obviously enjoying our astonished expressions. I beamed back, so glad to see her looking much better. She did look a bit thinner and more tired than usual but the same love of life was still there, it was pouring out of her at every angle. 'Look who I bumped in to in the corridor – Mr Portly!'

A roar erupted again. Mr Portly smiled round, then grabbed his handkerchief and dabbed at the corner of his eyes.

'I would like to say,' Mrs Fairchild's eyes became serious and we all automatically fell silent. 'That Detective Clifford has issued Mr Portly with an official apology, since the arrest of that awful Eddie Burrows he has been entirely cleared of any supposed wrong doing. It is my firm and unwavering view that we are very lucky to have Mr Portly as our deputy head.'

We all clapped and nodded solemnly while Mr Portly blew his nose.

'Detective Clifford has also asked me to present Diya Gala and Angel Anderson with official apologies for any distress and inconvenience caused,' Mrs Fairchild went on, retrieving two envelopes from a silk purse that she pulled out from under the cashmere blanket. 'He has also included vouchers to the best safari park in the country, knowing of their love of animals, so we will arrange for them to have a special outing there soon. Could Diya and Angel come up please?'

Diya and Angel collected their envelopes with pink cheeks and big smiles.

'And last but not least,' Mrs Fairchild's eyes twinkled again as she drew two more objects out of her silk purse. 'Detective Clifford has asked me to present these medals to the two aspiring detectives we have in the school, Davina Dupree and Arabella Rothsbury. He said he couldn't have solved the case without them. This is becoming something of a pattern, girls! You'll soon be enrolled with the local police force if you carry on like this.' Mrs Fairchild held out the medals and Arabella and I went up to collect them while Cleo and Clarice made sick noises behind us, pulling faces at us on the way back, earning themselves a sharp comment from Mrs Pumpernickle and a disappointed look from Mrs

Fairchild.

What an AMAZING DAY.COM! But there was one more surprise left...As Arabella and I walked down the squashy carpeted corridor towards our dorm, admiring our medals, Mrs Pumpernickle bustled up behind us.

'Post, Davina,' she said, pushing a thick envelope into my hands before hurrying off.

'Hmm,' I said, studying the postmark and swirly gold writing as Arabella pushed open our door. 'I think it's from my parents.'

'What, your crazy spy parents who probably work for the government but won't tell you for your own safety?' Arabella chuckled. 'I'm surprised they actually write letters, they usually send you messages disguised as other things don't they?'

'Yep,' I said, ripping it open and unfolding the thick cream paper. Last month they'd sent me a note stuffed into the inside of an expensive pen that arrived in a parcel, that said they hoped I was well and that they would be popping home briefly to do some washing before setting out on another secret mission. Marvellous! The month before that a carrier pigeon had dropped a bundle of sweets on my head while I was sitting in the school grounds with Arabella with a note that just said, "From M & D".

'It's definitely from my mum,' I said, looking at the unmistakable dramatic writing. 'I'll read it out. "Darling! Hope you are having a thrilling time at Egmont. Have you had time to take up those skydiving lessons I booked for you? Daddy and I have just escaped from a tricky situation in Columbia, can't say too much about it but I can say that we sat in the jungle for three days eating insects. Can you imagine?! Anyway Darling, we know it's your eleventh birthday next week so as a surprise we've booked two places on a luxury hot air balloon ride for you and a friend. Daddy's already cleared it with Mrs

Fairchild, she said you deserve a treat as you've been helping solve crimes or something – good girl – chip off the old block eh? Go to the website address at the bottom of this letter and enter the password "BIRTHDAY SURPRISE" and it will take you to the tickets, which you'll have to print off. And Darling, this is no ordinary hot air balloon ride so remember to bring a camera... Hugs and kisses, Mum xxx".'

Printed in Great Britain
by Amazon